Presented to

_____

from

_____

_____

_____ 19 _____

Dear Parents:

This book offers preschool children opportunities to learn and to review some basic safety lessons for outdoor play. Whether they are playing in a backyard, riding a bike, or at a playground, there are safety rules that are important for them to know. We think that your child may enjoy helping BJ learn and remember these safety lessons.

We consider books to be life-long gifts that develop and enhance the love of reading. Books are an excellent way to learn important information—like safety lessons—in a fun, entertaining way. We hope you enjoy reading along with Barney and BJ.

Mary Ann Dudko, Ph.D.
Margie Larsen, M.Ed.
Early Childhood Educational Specialists

Art Director: Tricia Legault
Designer: Jo Carol Arnold

©1996 The Lyons Group

PUBLISHING
A Division of The Lyons Group

300 East Bethany Drive, Allen, Texas 75002

The names and characters BARNEY, BABY BOP and BJ, and the BARNEY and star logo are trademarks of The Lyons Group.

1 2 3 4 5 6 7 8 9 10   98 97 96

ISBN 1-57064-073-4

Library of Congress Number 95-79185

Barney™ says, "Play Safely"

Written by Margie Larsen, M.Ed. and Mary Ann Dudko, Ph.D.
Illustrated by Bill Langley

BJ and Barney have a fun day planned at the park.

"Come on, Barney. Let's ride our bikes to the park," said BJ.

"That sounds great, BJ, but there's one thing we need to remember to be safe while riding our bikes," said Barney.

BJ looked puzzled and then smiled.
He remembered to put on his bike helmet.

"Now we're ready," said Barney.

BJ and Barney rode **safely** down the bike trail.
"Look. There's the park. Let's go!" said BJ excitedly.

"Wait, BJ. There's something we need
to remember before crossing the street,"
Barney reminded him.

BJ and Barney stopped at the stop sign.
They looked all around, looked around again,
then crossed the street.

BJ couldn't decide what to do first at the park.

Barney watched BJ swing,

then they played kickball.

"Look at the neat slide," said BJ.

"BJ, before you slide, we need to remember a way to be safe," said Barney.

BJ thought, and then remembered to slide down **feet first**.

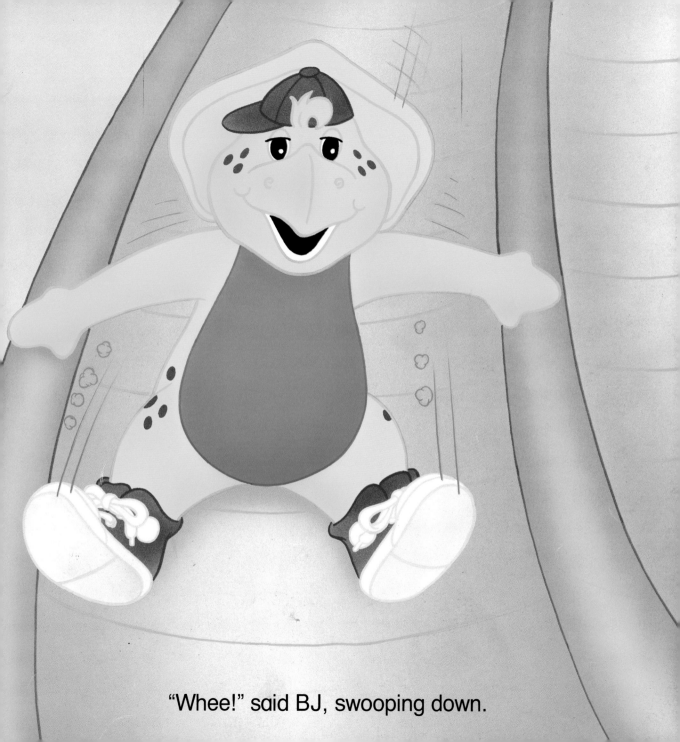

"Whee!" said BJ, swooping down.

Soon BJ and Barney were ready to leave.
"I'm ready," said BJ. "I remembered
to wear my bike helmet."

"That's good," said Barney. "But there's something else you need to do to be safe."

BJ looked up and down, then all around.

"Aye yie yie!" shouted BJ. "I need to tie my shoes!"

BJ and Barney rode their bikes to the edge of the street.
They both remembered to stop, look all around, and then
they rode carefully all the way home.

"Barney, thanks for going with me to the park today," said BJ. "I know one more thing to remember to be safe."

"What's that?" asked Barney.

BJ smiled and said, "Always have a friend with you.
It's safer that way, and a friend makes playing lots more fun!"